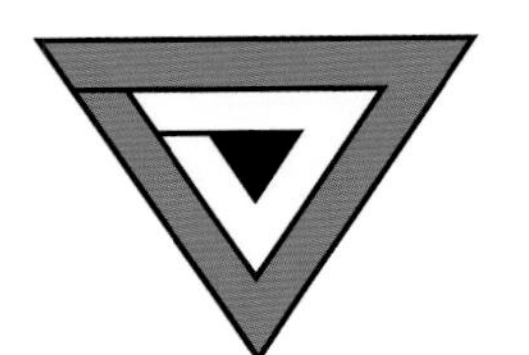
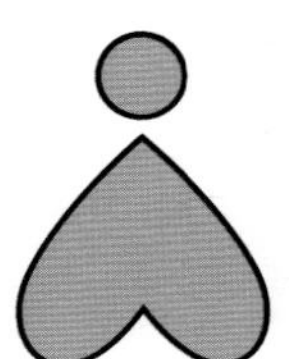

Visit us on the Web! rhcbooks.com

Educators and librarians, for a variety of teaching tools, visit us at RHTeachersLibrarians.com

Library of Congress Cataloging-in-Publication Data is available upon request.
ISBN 978-0-593-17508-8 (trade pbk.)
ISBN 978-0-593-17505-7 (hardcover)
ISBN 978-0-593-17506-4 (lib. bdg.)
ISBN 978-0-593-17507-1 (ebook)

The artist used Adobe Photoshop to create the illustrations for this book.
The text of this book is set in 11-point Sugary Pancake.
This edition's cover and interior design by Sylvia Bi and colorization by Sarah Stern

MANUFACTURED IN CHINA
10 9 8 7 6 5 4 3 2 1
First American Edition

Gavin Aung Than
Color by Sarah Stern

Random House New York

For Savannah

Chapter

Hi!
My name is
Junior Justice,
but you can
call me JJ.

I'm glad you received
my secret directions to this
warehouse for our meeting.

First, let
me just say a big
"thank you" to both
of you for coming.

I know this must have been hard for you.

But we're here because we're tired of being mistreated.

Tired of doing a thankless job.

Tired of being overshadowed and overworked.

Tired of being a sidekick.
You both know who my superhero partner is. He needs no introduction.
He is the most famous superhero in the world, after all.

Captain Perfect.
Well, away from the cameras . . .
. . . Captain Perfect is a complete jerk.

He makes me clean his secret headquarters every day.

Wash his costume after every battle. Do you know how hard it is to scrub alien bloodstains out?

And then he leaves me alone in his giant mansion while he's out taking all the credit!

Well, I've had **enough**!
I think we sidekicks should form our own **super team**. We don't need those adult heroes telling us what to do all the time.

Dinomite, Flygirl . . . **are you with me?**
You can count me in, mate.
My partner is an **unpredictable maniac!**

I've been Rampagin' Rita's sidekick ever since I started in the business.
RITA BASH!
BOOM
She means well, but all she wants to do is bash and clobber things.

Well, it's good to have you on board, Flygirl!

And what brings you here, Dinomite?
You must be a better leader than that buffoon Blast Radius.
Is it true you can transform into any dinosaur?
I also have a degree in quantum mechanics and can speak 47 languages.
But no one ever asks me about that.
Do you think you could . . . um . . . show us? Please?
Sigh . . . just this one time.
Name a dinosaur.

Velociraptor!
FHOOF!
Pterodactyl!
Technically not a dinosaur, but if you insist.
FHOOF!
Ankylosaurus!
FHOOF!
Triceratops!
FHOOF!

Brontosau–
FHOOF!
SMASH!

They never learn.
WHOA!

That was awesome. But what gives?
I thought your partner, Blast Radius, was pretty cool.
FHOOF!
HA HA HA!
More like a fool! Yes, I'm sure his leather jacket and muscles seem cool.
But Blast Radius is so one-dimensional.

He thought a gun-toting **Tyrannosaurus rex** was the ultimate weapon, so he strapped his silly missiles on me.
YAHOO!
It was **highly embarrassing**.
I've simply outgrown him, and I'm hoping this team of yours will provide me with a new challenge.

Yep, it will be a challenge.
But together, we can accomplish **anything!**
Together, no enemy will be **too great!** Together, we will ***PROTECT THE EARTH FROM—***
Um . . . excuse me?

Am late for meeting, yes?

GOO!
Dr. Enok's sidekick!
How did they find us?

Everyone, ATTACK!
CLICK
Where's Dr. Enok hiding? You two are never far apart.
Goo no hurt Junior Justice.

Goo just want to talk.
He's trying to trick us!
FHOOF!
I'm sure this is part of Dr. Enok's plan.
YAH!
No trick! No trick!

Please... let Goo speak.
Goo no hurt you.

No Dr. Enok. Goo promise.
Let Goo speak?

Okay, you've got one minute to explain yourself!
Fascinating substance.
Eww, gross.

Oh, thank you, Junior Justice!
Goo run away from Dr. Enok's evil lab.
Goo want to join sidekick team.

Let Dr. Enok's greatest creation join us?
I don't think so, buddy!

Yes, true. Dr. Enok create Goo in his laboratory.
PROJECT GOO

Yes, true, Goo his greatest creation.
Dr. Enok and Goo make good team. Even Captain Perfect and Junior Justice cannot stop us.
"Hey, you got lucky that time, pal!"

But Dr. Enok keep
Goo locked up in box.
He say
Goo too
dangerous
to be free.

Goo not like
being trapped.
Goo scared of dark.
Goo very, very
lonely.
So how did you escape?

Screw loose in jar. Goo can fit through
smallest hole. Easy for escape.

Please let Goo join team.
Goo scared to go back. Goo scared of box. Dr. Enok very bad man!
Goo sorry for past crimes.
Goo have no choice. Please! GOO JUST WANT FRIENDS!
Okay, okay! You can stay. Just get off me already.
Goo grateful. Goo thanks you all!
Aw, mate, you poor thing.
I always knew that Enok was a complete scoundrel.

Well then, we should mark our first official team meeting with a photo.
Ada, will you do the honors?
Image capture request confirmed.
Hmm, impressive tech.

Okay, everyone ready? Say "cheese" on three.
One, two, three...

CHEESE!

Chapter

What better way to celebrate our new team than with cookies? I baked them myself.
Oooh.
Delightful.

Aw, look. Goo's crying.
Goo so happy. Dr. Enok never bake cookies.

We can use this old warehouse as our headquarters.
Though we'll have to do something about that hole in the roof.

It needs a more refined sense of design. Perhaps a Victorian-era study with recliners and a fireplace.
I'll draw up some plans.
So what happens now, JJ?
Well, I thought we could show each other what we can do.
For instance, besides having expert cookie-making abilities, I'm also the world's greatest martial artist!

I've traveled the world learning all the **deadliest fighting styles.**
Kung fu. Karate.
Brazilian jujitsu.
Mongolian tickle fighting!

Mongolian tickle fighting? I've never heard of that.
Ah, it's perhaps the deadliest of them all. Allow me to demonstrate.

Hiyah!

Ha ha ha ha ha!
Stop! Stop!

Okay, I give up! I give up!

I think I peed a little.

My handy justice belt is full of crime-fighting gadgets.
Smoke bombs, stun grenades, electronic trackers, lollipops, you name it.

And, of course, you've met Ada. She's the most advanced computer in the world.
Pleasure to meet you all!
Especially you, Flygirl.
According to my data, you are the world's most acrobatic flyer.
Gee, mate, I don't like to brag . . .

. . . but yeah, I guess I'm pretty agile!
Wow!
Goo like!
Plus I carry these bug balls for attacking criminals.
I have a bug for every battle scenario.

Fighting crime with bugs?

That sounds pretty weak, if you ask me.

I mean, with all due respect to Flygirl, how on earth are **teeny-tiny bugs** going to stop a super criminal?
I just don't think it's very . . .

. . . effective.

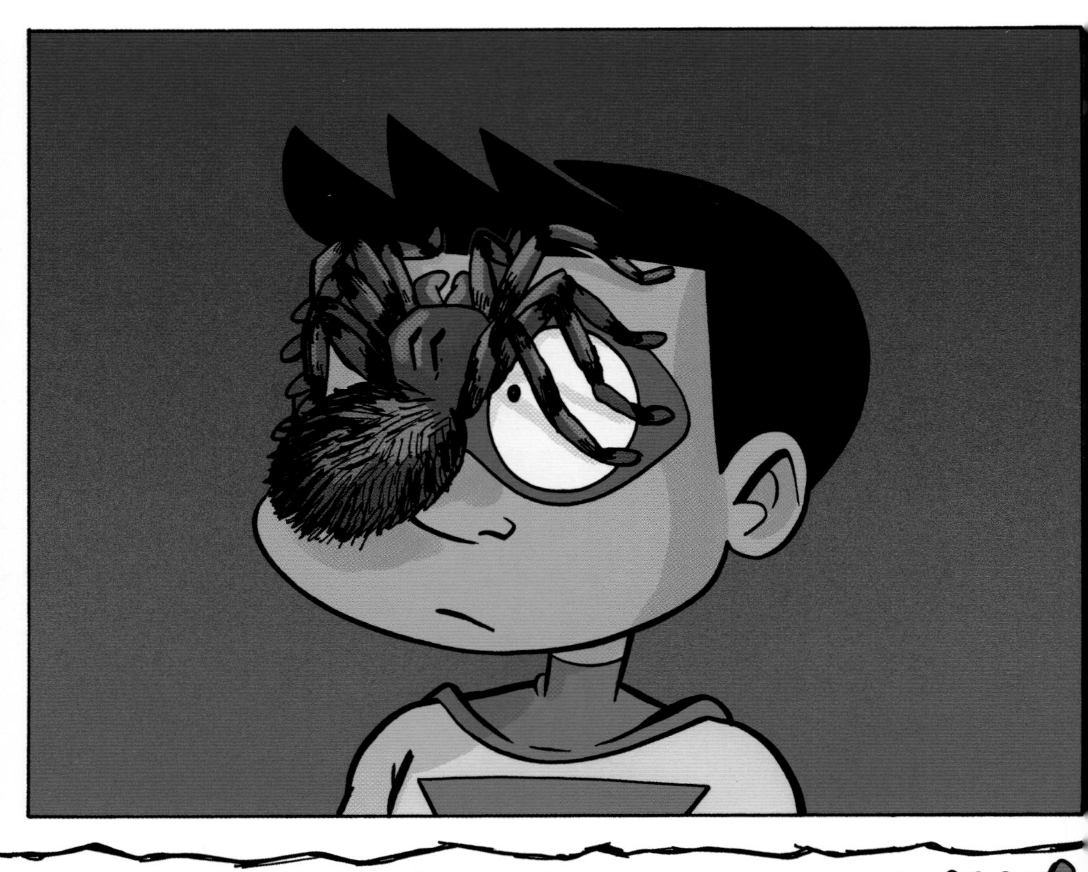
AAAAAAAAAAAAAAAAAHHHHHHHHH!

Very effective.

Get it off! Get it off!

I stand corrected, Flygirl. I'll never pick a fight with you again.

The Goliath bird-eating spider. Native to South America.
While its venom is relatively harmless, it does pack a nasty bite.

They're the largest spiders in the world. And also the cutest, if you ask me.

Back into your ball, little fella.
That thing is so gross.

What about you, Goo? You've already shown us how formidable you are, but **what exactly** are your powers?

Goo nervous. Goo never audition for super team before.

Don't be nervous, mate. You can be yourself around us.

Goo have no powers.
Goo is just . . . Goo!

Goo
like to express
Goo-self.
Sometimes
Goo like
flat.

Sometimes . . .
WHOOSH!

Goo like big.
Amazing.

Whatever Goo feel like, Goo do. Not think much about it.

I don't think you know how powerful you are, buddy.
Goo just happy to be here. With friends.

Dinomite turn now?
Hey, where is Dinomite?

You've already seen what I can do. I put a hole in the roof of our headquarters, remember?
Now, please, I'm trying to work. **Gravity and quantum theory** aren't going to unify themselves.
PHYSICS

Uh, what?
Must I explain everything?
A unified theory of the universe. I'm determined to be the first dinosaur to solve it.
STRING THEORY

Okaaaaay, we'll just leave you to it.

This is so nice.
Just being able to relax and not worry about Rampagin' Rita dropping a building on me.

I know, it's great without Captain Perfect around forcing me to—

JUNIOR JUSTICE!
Oh no.

We've been looking everywhere for you.

Chapter

Thank goodness I found you, Junior Justice! I need you back at the mansion **right now.**
My laundry needs to be done, and Super Mutt hasn't been taken for a walk yet.

Didn't you get the letter I left you?

Letter? I normally have you read my fan mail.

Well, allow me to clarify. **I quit as your sidekick!**
I'm sick of you treating me like your personal assistant.
We sidekicks are forming our **own team**. We don't need you adults anymore.
HA HA HA
HA HA HA HA

Hee hee, ha ha, hoo hoo.
Good one, Junior Justice.

Wait, you're serious?
Very.

But who's gonna wash my clothes, cook my food, clean my headquarters, cut my toenails, and scrub my toilet?
It's always about you, isn't it?
Of course!
I'm Captain Perfect, the most beloved person in the world, after all.

You no want to be Rita sidekick?
I'm sorry, Rampagin' Rita. We had some good adventures together, but it's time I moved on.

But we have fun BASHING things together.
You bashed everything! I just tried to stay out of your way.

You making Rita angry. You wouldn't like it when Rita get angry.
I'm not changing my mind.

This can't be true, little dude! We make the coolest team.
I hated every second of it.

No way, man! Didn't you like strapping on my missile launchers and blowing away bad guys?

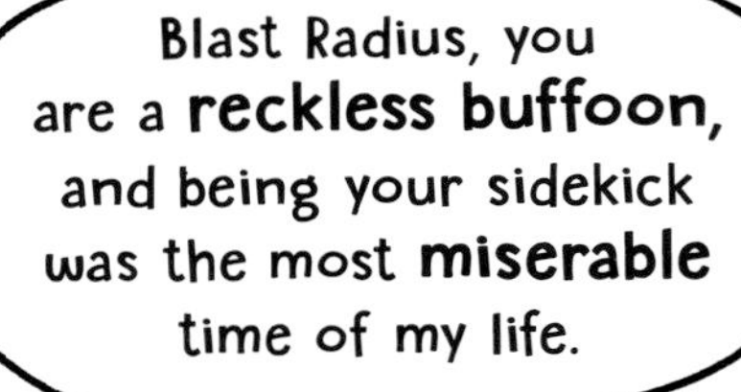
Blast Radius, you are a **reckless buffoon,** and being your sidekick was the most **miserable** time of my life.

Good day, sir!

Gee, harsh, man.

Look, this was a nice little stunt, kids, but I've had enough of this nonsense.
C'mon, Junior Justice, let's go home.
Don't you get it, Captain? **We're not going back, ever!**
Why don't we discuss this after you've cooked me a nice . . .
Hmm, that's strange.
Pink's a weird color for a warehouse wall. And the paint's still wet.
Captain Perfect, that not paint . . .

That GOO!
Heh . . . nice to meet you.
RITA BASH!
BOOM!

It's **blasting** time!
PHOOM!
PHOOM!
PHOOM!
Don't shoot!

Dude!

What are you doing? He's one of the **bad guys!**
No, he's not!
Just let us explain.

Where's
Dr. Enok hiding,
scumbag?
Aaaah!
Slippery
devil!
Move!
I've got my blaster set
to vaporize!
No,
stop attacking!

Why are you protecting that thing?
Goo evil creature. Must be bashed!
Goo's changed! He's on our new team.

Excuse me?!
BASH HIM GOOD!

Captain Perfect, Rampagin' Rita, and Blast Radius, YOUR ATTENTION PLEASE!

I was trying to get some work done before you three so rudely interrupted.
Now I'm going to have to ask you to—

Leave.

Suddenly very sleepy . . .

Night-night time.
FHOOF!

Dinomite!
He's out cold.
I have to say, my feelings are hurt.

You threw a party and didn't invite **me**.
DR. ENOK!

I don't know what you're up to, Enok, but I won't let you fly out of here in one piece.

He's not going back with you, Enok!
Goo told us about all the **abuse** you've inflicted on him over the years.
Yeah, he won't be yours to torture any longer.
Abuse? Torture? **Nonsense!** I am Goo's creator.
He is mine to treat as I see fit.
Now step aside, children . . .

ZKKKK
. . . you're in over your head.

ZAP!

GOO!
WHOOSH!
It was my fault for letting you escape, my pet. My containment device wasn't strong enough.
I won't be making that mistake again.
GLOOP!

NO MORE BOX! NO MORE BOX!
Ada, get me up there.
Roger, Junior Justice. Initiating glider control.
3, 2, 1 . . .
Alley-oop!

Junior Justice, what are you doing? Goo's not worth it!
Ah, the idealistic nature of youth. Full of so much futile purpose.
I'll get you out of there, buddy!
Oopsie.
Nice try, but that container is made from an adamankium alloy. It's unbreakable.
OUCH!

Look, this newfound friendship is all very **touching**. But my patience is starting to wear thin.

Goo, it's time to return to the lab and—

What the?

OW!

That's an Arizona bark scorpion. Victims say their sting feels like a thousand tiny electric shocks.
Goo stays here with us, where he belongs.

ARGH!
Enough of this!

ATTACK.
ATTACK THEM ALL!

RITA BASH!
Eat laser, robot trash!
Don't touch the hair!
Ah, I love the smell of burnt robot in the—
Hey, give that back!

Nice shot, JJ.
Not bad yourself, Flygirl!
THONK!
DIE, PUNY ROBOT!

AHHH!
ZZAAAAK!
There are too many of them!
Get off me, you glorified tin can!
NO!
JJ, they've got Goo!

Captain Perfect, you have to save Goo!
This has gone far enough, Junior Justice. Goo is a villain.
I don't help villains.
He's one of us, I swear!
Please, Captain, I'm begging you.
SAVE HIM!
I don't know what's gotten into you, Junior Justice . . .

. . . but those two deserve each other.
FRIENDS!

Chapter

Ugh, what did I miss?
You could have saved him!
Why should I save an evil villain?
Why Flygirl angry?
Yeah, chill out, little lady.
Goo was our friend!

Can everyone please stop shouting? I have a tyrannosaur-sized headache.
Sorry, Dinomite.
But you just missed Goo getting kidnapped by Dr. Enok, and Captain Perfect not lifting a finger to stop it.
It's not my fault you three have gone completely nuts!

First, you want to quit being our sidekicks.
And as if that's not bad enough, now you want to help Dr. Enok's crony?
How many times do I have to say it? Goo's not evil anymore!
He's one of us now, a good guy.
I enjoy his company better than the likes of you three.
I've had enough of this. If you really want to stop being our sidekicks, then it's fine with us!

FINE!

FINE!

FINE!

FINE!

FINE!

Um . . .

It's your turn to say "fine."
Oh.

FINE!

You'll never make it on your own.
I bet you'll come crawling back to us!
We'll take our chances.
Let's go, chums . . .
. . . I grow tired of these **three nincompoops.**
FHOOF!

You know the best thing about our team?
What's that?

No adults allowed.

BYE!

Where are you taking us, Dinomite?
Just follow me. I know a place we can go.
The Opera House?

I always come here when I need to get away from Blast Radius. It's a good place to think.

Wow, you can see the **whole city** from up here.
Yes, quite breathtaking, isn't it?

What's wrong, JJ? You're missing the view.
How are we meant to protect this city when we can't even protect our teammate?

Maybe Captain Perfect is **right**.
Maybe we're not cut out to make it on our own.
Maybe we're better off just being sidekicks.
What are you talking about?

We haven't even been a team for **one day** and we've already had our **headquarters destroyed** and let one of our members get **kidnapped**.

Just a minor hiccup, chum. Nothing we can't figure out.
We don't even have a team name yet!

We can worry about that later. We've got our first mission to complete.
Huh? What do you mean?

Rescue Goo, of course!
Rescue Goo?

Goo's our mate, and we **never, ever leave a mate behind**. He risked his life to escape Dr. Enok, and now he's his prisoner again.
Who knows what that evil maniac is doing to him!
Yes, I agree.

Dr. Enok is the **world's greatest criminal,** with an army of robot drones at his command.

I don't know if we can beat him.

Quit doubting yourself, JJ. We wouldn't have joined your team if we didn't believe in you.
But we don't even know where Enok is.
The location of his laboratory is a complete mystery.

Junior Justice, allow me to interrupt.

I went to the trouble of placing a tracker on Dr. Enok in the middle of our altercation.

I'm getting a signal on his whereabouts. A remote island approximately 89 miles southeast of here.
Oh, sweet Ada, I could kiss you!
You really think we can do this?
It's what mates do for each other!
We owe it to Goo to give it a jolly good try.

All right, if you two are in, then so am I.
You bet I'm in!
As am I, chums.
Hold on, Goo . . .
WE'RE ON OUR WAY!

Chapter

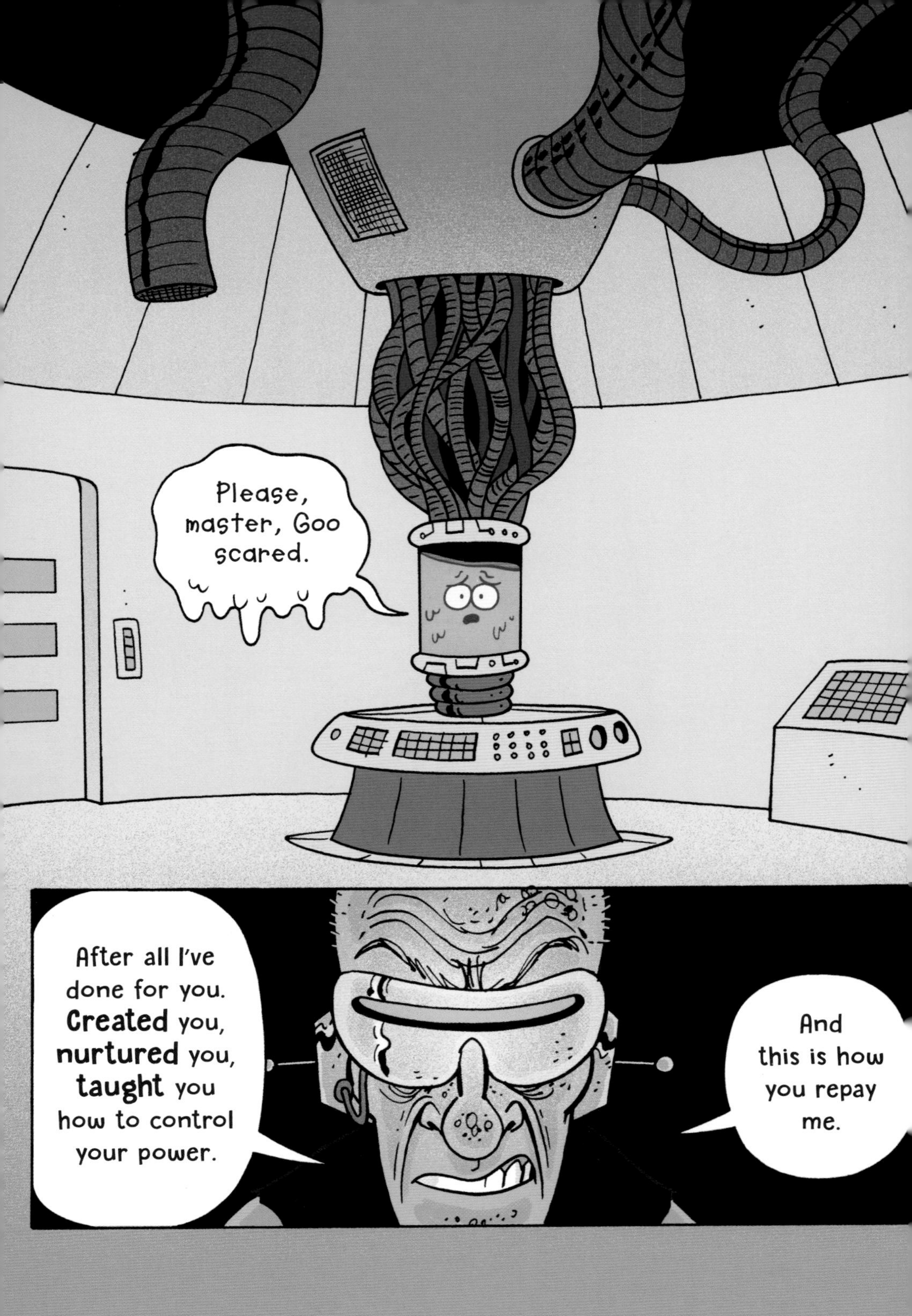
Please, master, Goo scared.
After all I've done for you. **Created** you, **nurtured** you, **taught** you how to control your power.
And this is how you repay me.

By leaving me to join those . . . those . . . I can barely say the word: "heroes."
I'm afraid I can't let that go unpunished.
TREMOR: LOW
WRRRRRRR
WAAAH!
UGH. Goo don't feel so good.
Yes, my discombobulator will leave you woozy.
You see, I built it to put your one weakness to the test: vibrations.

Here, allow me to demonstrate it to you again.
TREMOR: HIGH
WRRRRRR
ARGH!
Please, master. No more shaking.
Goo promise no run away again.
GOO SORRY!

Hmm, you call that an apology?
TREMOR: HIGHER

WRRRRRRRRRR

I've always been curious about how much discombobulation you can withstand before your molecules break down.
You seem to be reaching your limit.

Gck gck tch.

TREMOR: HIGHEST

But you know what? I designed you to be **durable**.

TREMOR: EXTREME!

I think you can take a little more.
WRRRRRRR
E
AAAAAAAAAH!

There it is!
Dr. Enok's lab.
Let's hope we're not too late.

We would have gotten here sooner if Dinomite hadn't stopped for **fish and chips**.
I don't like to fight supervillains on an empty stomach.

So what's the plan, JJ?
Flygirl, see if you can find a way in from the roof. Once you get inside, look for Goo.

Dinomite and I will create a diversion to buy you some time.
How will you do that?
I've got something up my sleeve.
Got it, I'll see you inside. Good luck, you two!

This air vent looks like it leads down to the lab. But, gee, it's pretty gross in there.

Ah, quit complaining, girl. Goo needs you!

Nice of Dr. Enok to throw us a party celebrating the return of his precious pet.
Not sure about his choice of music, though.
OIL
OIL

AAAAAAAAAAAAAHHHHHH!
That's not music. That's Goo getting discombobulated.
E
WELCOME
GOO

BOOM!
What on earth? Something's trying to breach the lab!

Hurry, we must notify Dr. E—

—noooooooooooook!
GREETINGS, CHUMS!
KA-CRASH!

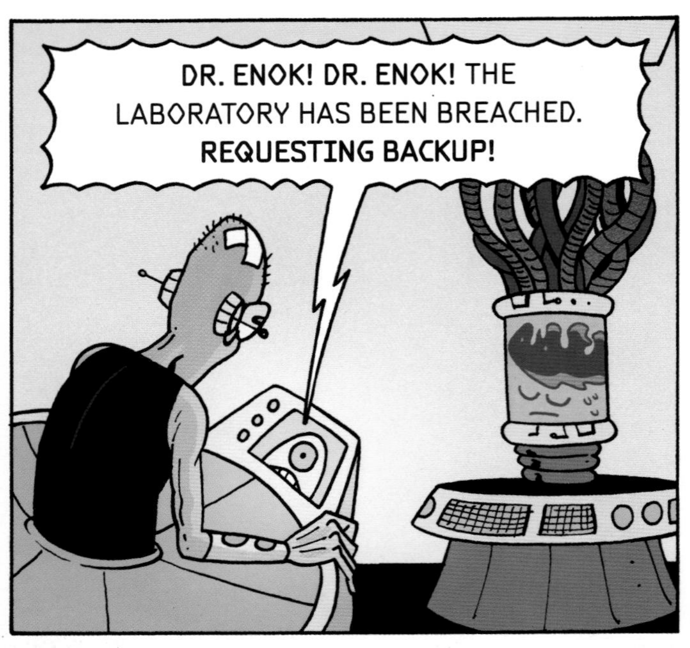
DR. ENOK! DR. ENOK! THE LABORATORY HAS BEEN BREACHED. REQUESTING BACKUP!

Ah, isn't that cute, Goo? Your little sidekick comrades have arrived.

Excellent, this gives me a chance to test out my new invention.

Coast is clear!

Goo, wake up! *WAKE UP!*
Oh, mate, you don't look so good.

Don't worry. I'm going to get you out of there.

These **trap-jaw ants** have some of the most **powerful pincers** in the animal kingdom.

They should be able to burrow into the computer circuitry . . .

. . . and bite through the electrical cables.

Strange.
Dr. Enok's
defenses aren't
as strong as
I thought they
would be.
I was expecting
more resistance.
THOOM

I trust that this satisfies your expectations?
Oh my!
Dinomite, allow **me** to handle this.

Junior Justice? You're . . . you're a giant!
That's right, Doc. I finally had a **growth spurt!**

What . . . what sort of trickery is this?

The only trick I know is how to kick an evil old man's butt without breaking a sweat.
Allow me to demonstrate.
Bah, this doesn't change anything. I will crush you no matter how big you are.

WHAT?

There's nothing there!

It's a hologram.
Amazing. The imagery is so lifelike.
I must have this technology.
GIVE IT TO ME NOW!
Sorry, Doc, Ada is all mine.
NOW, DINOMITE!

Jolly good!
SMASH!
Thanks, Ada. Your new hologram app worked great.
You are most welcome, Junior Justice.
Grahhh, I grow tired of these games!
FHOOF!

Yes, it worked! The ants short-circuited the computer lock.

C'mon, Goo, time to get outta here.

GOO! What's wrong with you, mate?

INTRUDER! INTRUDER!
HEY, GET YOUR HANDS OFF ME!

GOO!
HELP,
HELP!
WAKE UP!
WE NEED
YOU!
YOUR
FRIENDS
NEED YOU!

This has gone on long enough.
You are mere sidekicks, after all.
CRASH
FLICK
FHOOF!
Junior Justice, I think it's past your bedtime.

Come, let me put you to sleep.
DOCTOR! I found this one snooping around in your chamber.
Ah, yes, the pretty young . . . insect.
You know, my child, when I was your age, there was nothing I enjoyed more than pulling the wings off flies.
Having the power in my fingertips to take away the very thing that makes something so special . . .

. . . filled me with such **happiness**.
Please, not my wings. **Anything but my wings!**

Ah, I feel like a boy again.
AAAAIIIIIEEEEE!
MASTER!

Put
Goo friend
down.

How did you escape? Get back in your box. I'll deal with you later.
Goo said **put friend** down!

Sigh. Do you really think you're better off with these foolish sidekicks?

Do you truly think you're going to survive in the real world without me to protect you?
I dreamed you into existence. Created you out of nothing but my own genius.
YOU ARE A PART OF ME!
Do you think these children know you like I know you?
Care about you like I care about you?
Love you like I love you?

NOW GET BACK INTO YOUR BOX!

NO MORE BOX!

I SAID GET BACK INTO YOUR—

SLOOP!

Goo?

NO.
MORE.

Uh-oh.

BOX!

NO.

MORE.

BOX!

No more box.
Ugh, my lab.
My beautiful lab.

You betrayed me. After everything I've done for you!
All of you worthless sidekicks will pay for this!
You hear me? Dr. Enok will have his
REVEEEEEEEEEENNNGE!

GOO!
Well, chum . . .

. . . remind me **never** to make you angry.
Goo cannot believe friends come for him.

You're a part of the team, remember?
Yeah, friends don't leave each other behind.

So happy. Goo cry now.

C'mere, ya big blob.
Gimme a hug!

Aw, Dinomite,
are you crying, too?
Of course
not . . .

. . . my tear
ducts involuntarily leak
from time to time.

Chapter

You have to admit, we work pretty well together.

You two should have seen Dinomite smashing Dr. Enok's entire robot army. It was awesome!

Well, that hologram ruse you tricked Enok with was quite a sight to behold.

Flygirl use ants to rescue Goo from box. So cool!

Look who's talking, mate. What you did was incredible.
Did you know you had so much power?

No, Goo never do that before.
So angry. Goo just lose control.

I'm just
glad you're on
our side.
But what do we do now?
We still don't have a team name.
Or a
headquarters.

FOUND
THEM!

Oh great, you three again.
Look, we're **not** going back to being your sidekicks, and that's that.
Relax, kids, we're not trying to make you come back.
Although are you sure you don't want to do my laundry? I have a huge pile of filthy capes that needs washing.
NO!

Fine.
Listen, we and the rest of the superhero community heard what happened. That you defeated Dr. Enok and his robot army.
Your hair . . . it seems to **defy gravity**. Can I take a sample for analysis?
Sorry, friend. Under no circumstances does anyone touch my perfect hair.

Heck, dudes, we even heard you destroyed Enok's lab.
GOOD BASHING!

We can't take credit for destroying the lab. **That was all Goo.**
Are you ready to believe he's a good guy now?

Yes, we're willing to accept that young Goo is on our side now.

But I'll be keeping a very close eye on him.

And we're sorry about the way things ended back in the warehouse. We should have had more faith in you and your abilities.
Is there anything we can do to make it up to you? Maybe buy you some pizza?

I can teach you how to blast things!

Rita bash something for you?

Well . . .
. . . there is one thing you could use your super awesome powers to help us with.
Rita ready!
Right on, bro!
You name it, Junior Justice!
Can you help build our new headquarters?
Um . . .

And so, a few days later . . .
Huff puff.
Okay, this is the last of the scrap metal from Dr. Enok's lab.
Where should I put it?
Just follow Ada's directions. She'll show you where to place everything.
Materials for top exterior walls and windows. Proceed to *27th floor.*

Perfect.
Do you think we're being too mean?
Well, they offered to help, and Captain Perfect's super strength and speed are being put to good use.

Yes, thanks to them, my design will be complete in a few days instead of years.

Okay, maybe it's a little mean.
HEE HEE
HEE HEE
HEE
HEE HEE HEE

Okay, Junior Justice . . . All done.
Thanks so much to all of you!
We're . . . we're going to take a nap now.
ZZZZZZZZZZZ
It's absolutely fantastic!

Goo love new home!
Wow, you designed this all by yourself, Dinomite?
I like to dabble in architecture and engineering in my spare time.

Awesome, a training room to practice martial arts!
And a room for all my bugs!
This is my library, filled with the complete works of the greatest writers and thinkers in history.
All first editions, I might add.

And for you, Goo, no more little box to be trapped in. This giant empty room is yours.
You can stretch and expand all you want here.
WHEEEEE!
Thank you, thank you, thank you!

I hope you don't mind, but I went to the trouble of choosing our team name.
Ada, it should be on your hard drive.
Ah, yes, allow me.
Excellent, Dinomite! Criminals all over the world will learn to fear these words.
It honors our past but adds a cool new twist. I love it.
Goo cannot read!
Let me spell it out for you, buddy.
There's a new superhero team in town, and they're called the . . .

SUPER SIDEKICKS

To be continued . . .

GAVIN'S DRAWING TIPS

START WITH SIMPLE SHAPES FIRST: For instance, JJ is just made of circles and rectangles.

DON'T DRAW TOO DARK: Sketch lightly until you get the basic structure right.

ONE STEP AT A TIME: Once you have the structure done, it's time to draw all the cool details.

JUST HAVE FUN: Don't worry if you think you're not getting it right. Keep practicing—it takes time to get good!

DRAW JJ

DRAW FLYGIRL

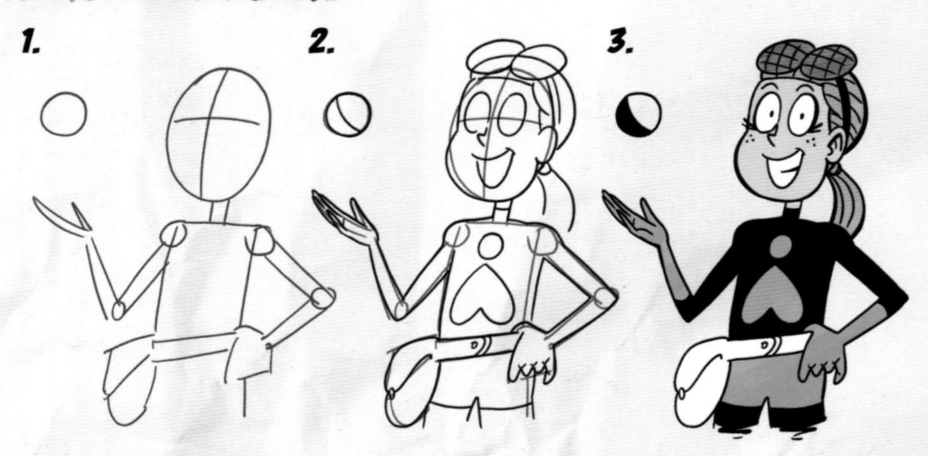

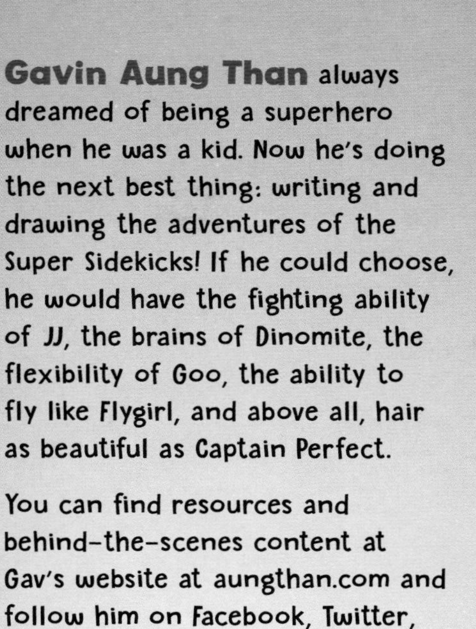

Gavin Aung Than always dreamed of being a superhero when he was a kid. Now he's doing the next best thing: writing and drawing the adventures of the Super Sidekicks! If he could choose, he would have the fighting ability of JJ, the brains of Dinomite, the flexibility of Goo, the ability to fly like Flygirl, and above all, hair as beautiful as Captain Perfect.

You can find resources and behind-the-scenes content at Gav's website at aungthan.com and follow him on Facebook, Twitter, and Instagram at @zenpencils.

The Super Sidekicks will return in their next amazing adventure!

The Mother of the Seas is sick of humans using the oceans as a junkyard, so she decides to give the land dwellers a taste of their own medicine. Prepare for an unbelievable underwater menace that threatens to destroy the entire world in . . .

Super Sidekicks Book Two:

OCEAN'S REVENGE